A FRIEND FOR MERIDA

By Irene Trimble

Illustrated by Massimiliano Narciso, Elsa Chang, and Grace Lee

Random House New York

ISBN: 978-0-7364-2904-7
randomhouse.com/kids
Printed in the United States of America

10 9 8 7 6 5 4 3

It was a beautiful day in the Highlands, perfect for a ride in the woods. Princess Merida ran happily into the castle stable.

"Angus!" she called. But her beloved horse and best friend was nowhere to be found.

Finally, Merida spotted Angus outside. He was helping the stable master carry a load of stones near the edge of a very high bridge.

"Uh-oh," said Merida, hurrying toward her friend.

Merida knew that although Angus was big and powerful, even he got frightened at times.

He **spooked** at loud noises.

He was **scared** of the dark.

And he **really** did not like heights.

When Merida arrived at the bridge, Angus was **rearing and bucking.**

Merida flung her arms around Angus to calm him down.
"Ah, you're fine now, lad!" she said, soothing
the big horse.

Merida led Angus away, and the two raced joyfully into the hills beyond the castle.

Feeling free, they went farther from home than either of them had dared to go before.

As the afternoon light began to fade, Merida and Angus came
across an old road that led into a dark, misty wood.

"An adventure!" Merida said excitedly. She patted
Angus to encourage him. "Shall we have a look?"

They passed a crumbling stone tower and the **spooky** remains of an ancient manor.

The mist thickened and the forest became darker.
Merida decided it was time to head for home.

But as she turned Angus around, Merida saw a huge
shadowy figure looming over her.

"What is it?" Merida whispered, trying to see more clearly. "Could it be a bear? Or is it a ghost?"

Slowly, she pulled out her bow . . . just in case.

Suddenly, a twig snapped.

Angus jumped sideways,
nearly throwing Merida to the ground.
"It's only a bird!" the princess called out.
But Angus was too startled to listen. With a
frightened whinny, he took off like a shot.

Angus charged wildly ahead. As the horse bolted
out of the glen, the fog lifted, and Merida saw that the towering
figure behind them was just an old tree.

Merida struggled to grab Angus's reins to slow him down.
Angus raced forward—toward the edge of a cliff!
Merida pulled back desperately on her horse's reins.

"No, Angus! Stop!" Merida shouted. But it was too late—they were about to tumble over the edge!

Just then, Merida spotted a ledge on the opposite side of the ravine. It was very far away.

Merida leaned forward and hugged her friend.

"Angus!" she said. "You need to jump! I have full faith in you."

Merida and Angus reached the cliff's edge.
Angus was terrified, but he trusted
his best friend and knew she believed in him.

Angus didn't stop. With every ounce of
his strength, the horse leaped high
into the air, sailed across the
ravine—

—and **landed safely** on the other side!

Angus didn't stop running
until he and Merida were back
at the castle.

Safe at home, Merida felt a surge of love as she hugged Angus. Believing and trusting in each other had saved them both.

As she gazed contentedly at the big horse, Merida knew that she and Angus would be best friends for life.